THE LEGENDS SERIES

THE LEGENDS SERIES

Book 1: The Beginning

Solber Martinez

Rev. date: 04/10/2013

To order additional copies of this book, contact:
Xlibris Corporation
1-888-795-4274
www.Xlibris.com
Orders@Xlibris.com
132773

CONTENTS

I dedicate this book to my family, my teachers, my fifth-grade teacher Mrs. Aivazis for getting me to start writing, and Danica Cheremnov for helping me to push on.

PROLOGUE

David and Jake ran across the cracked ground. "Faster!" David yelled as Jake jogged far behind David. *CRACKLE! BOOM!* The ground exploded, and another hole appeared. David made a twister with his staff and shot it at a flying group of Dark mages. David and Jake halted to rest. They shot mini tornadoes and balls of lightning at the sky and ground. As they fought, mages flew toward them.

"Have you cleared the skies yet?" one of them asked.

"Obviously not, haven't you noticed there are still explosions and mortals running for their boring lives?" said David.

The mages just flew off. As they did, David said, "*Light!*" A golden ball shot out of David's staff. KABOOM! David yelled triumphantly until the Dark King Landor appeared. He choked David and Jake with a Dark Energy Rope.

"The Third War . . . what a terrible time to die," said Landor and started sucking the life out of the two . . .

CHAPTER 1

The Dark's Plan

MANY MONTHS AGO . . .

The Dark King Landor walked across the hallway of his enormous palace, his black robes flapping behind him, his shoes clicking on the marble floor. Landor walked to a pair of double doors and opened them. Inside were a small chest and a torch, lighting up the small room. Landor opened the chest and found a scroll tinted green and covered in dust. Someone came into the room.

"My king, the Dark Spell mages have arrived. They are waiting in the throne room. They are ready for the spell," said the man. The Dark King Landor nodded. "My king, can you explain to me why we are doing this again?" the man asked. Landor turned around, facing the man.

"A mage who lives on Earth is a history teacher at the Dijenuks' school. He is a light fire mage, and he has the book titled *The Legends*. When the book is opened, all the Elemental Crystals will disappear and reappear at their Elemental Chamber. All of us may lose the Elements but not the Dark Element. I hired the most powerful Spell mages in the Dark side, so they will enchant the Dark Crystal so it won't disappear with the rest. They will also curse the mage on Earth to make him open *The Legends*. We will find the Elemental Crystals, put them in the Dark Shrine so the Light won't get the powers, and we will take them over. We won't take the Light Crystal though . . . I have . . . plans for that one. The first Element we will find is the Wind Element. This plan may backfire, however. The Agreement of the Elementian War says that when the book is opened at any time other than the Legends Ceremony, then three wars are made between Light and Dark," explained Landor.

The man nodded. "Yes, my king, but what about the Dijenuks?" asked the man.

"Those two are the last in their family, except for maybe . . . Bertank Dijenuk. I would order my men to kill him later but at the right time. I already have the first scroll here in my hands. The second one is close to one of my prisons on the Light side. The third scroll is with Bertank, and he lives on Earth, hiding near a governmental prison. I sent a boy to the Dijenuks' school to stop them and trap them in the school while it's being destroyed. If they still live, someone will pick up the Dijenuks and bring them to Camp Dijenuk, where they will gain their staff and learn about their fate. A group of Dark mages will attack Camp Dijenuk and steal their shrine so they won't be able to put the Elemental Crystals there. Of course, they will get the shrine back. That's why I'm putting it in a close-by area. Once they get it back, the mages will attack them and bring them to a prison, and I don't know which one. Before that, though, I'll have some more mages capture them, after which they will be rescued, come back, look for the shrine, and get captured once more like I have said. I will send a mage to create a portal to send some government officials from a place called the United States. These government officials will capture the mages in the prison when the Light side tries to save them, and they will fight in a place on Earth called . . . Area 51. There, the dark side, light side, and the United States government will fight. One of the Dijenuks, who has visions of the future, will have a vision of a man who supposedly kills him. That Dijenuk, who is weak from an explosion, will send the other Dijenuks after that man. The Dijenuk will fall into a pit where the Dijenuk named Bertank lives. I will go back to the battle and send the Light side back to Elektia, leaving Jake alone in the area. The Dark side will leave, and the government will run away. Then . . . well, that's all I can explain for now. Let's go, those Spell mages are waiting for me." Landor left the room with the man.

At the end of the hallway, Landor opened another door leading to a spiral staircase. They went down the staircase and opened another door. They went through winding tunnels, leading to large doors. Landor opened one, revealing a large room with a red carpet and one large throne. Landor sat on the throne and faced three women wearing white robes with cuffs tinted black. The three women bowed.

"Now, I assume you three are the most powerful Spell mages in the Dark side, correct?" asked Landor. The three women nodded. "I want to curse a man named Barbeck Wakigoober. He lives in a place called Seattle, Washington, United States. I want him to open a book called *The Legends.*

That's all I will tell you," said Landor, who was clearly afraid to tell them too much information.

The three women nodded. One raised a long pole made of black wood. "A triple-point triangle!" she commanded. The second stood about two feet to the side of the first. The third stood behind both of them. They raised their poles and whispered a few words. There was a faint *boom*, and the tips of the poles glowed white. Landor grinned.

"Well done. In about two hours, the curse will take effect just as I had planned. Soon, I will rule Elektia and Earth and conquer the universe!"

The women left the throne room. Landor laughed. "Yes, my plan is working, and my brothers and cousins said I could not be successful! I want to prove them wrong! I want to kill the Dijenuk family!" There was the sound of the thunder, and light-years away, Bertank Wakigoober fell to the ground.

His mind spun, and he got dizzy. He stumbled as he got up and opened a locked chest under his bed. He opened it and found a rotting old book inside of it, titled *The Legends*, and on the cover was a shining *D* with colored dots around it. With the book in his hands, he got ready for work and drove to a middle school on a rainy day. He passed a lot of houses on his way. Bertank Dijenuk and the people of the city didn't know that in one of those houses, two boys were getting ready to go to school, where they would start an adventure. These boys lived ordinary lives in an ordinary house. The only problem was that they had no other family members, except for their stepparents.

These boys did not know that there was a distant world where the people could do magical things, both good and evil. They did not know that their family was powerful. They did not know that their family was honored. They did not know that they soon had to save this distant planet and Earth as well. They did not know that they had to find a family secret, one where all questions would be answered.

These boys were David Dijenuk and Jake Dijenuk, who were cousins. David's father was a Dijenuk who married someone who took the name Dijenuk after the marriage. Jake's mother was also 100 percent Dijenuk. David and Jake were cousins, and they were the last members of the Dijenuk family.

CHAPTER 2

Destruction

Sometimes, people keep important secrets from us, people such as our family. Two cousins face something dangerous involving the secret of their family. Their adventure starts suddenly and unexpectedly. Reader, be prepared—this is The Legends Series.

David and Jake Dijenuk had no idea what their fates would lead to. David was a bit tall, with dark hair and brown eyes, and he was a bit of a troublemaker. Jake, however, had brown hair. They thought all was well.

"Get your backpack, Jake!" yelled Oka Stert, David and Jake's stepmom. They had the same stepparents even though the two boys were cousins and not brothers. Their stepfather, Steve, was giving them their lunch.

"All right, umm . . . is that all?" Steve asked.

David nodded.

Jake checked his lunch. "Thanks, Mom, I love rice pudding!" he said. Jake didn't know, but that rice pudding would be his last.

David then checked his own lunch. "Yes, I got pound cake!" said David in excitement.

Many years ago, David's parents were murdered for an unknown reason, then minutes later, Jake's parents were also murdered mysteriously. No one knew who did it or why. A family member named Uncle Bertank brought the two three-year-old boys to Steve and Oka. Two months later, Bertank died of cancer, and David and Jake became the last members of their family—the Dijenuks. Even now, the two wondered about their parents, but that didn't stop them from having a happy life.

Steve drove the two kids to their middle school. The two liked their city; it was close to Oregon, but they lived in Seattle, Washington. It was raining, of course, but not as hard as usual. Their school was fairly large, with two floors and many classrooms.

"Hey, David, ready for another D in history?" said a kid called Gerardo, an intelligent but rather rude eighth grader who always made fun of David. Gerardo was also David and Jake's classmate in history class. He always made fun of him for not being ordinary. The two had no idea why they were called unordinary.

David Dijenuk was just an ordinary seventh grader, or at least he thought so. He didn't really refer himself as different.

"November 28 and we already have—almost literally—tons of homework," said David to his (strangely) only cousin, Jake Dijenuk. He was one of those A students.

"Well, it looks pretty easy!" said Jake as they walked to first period.

"Easy for you, brainy," said David, smirking a little as the two walked into the classroom for history.

Mr. Wakigoober, who was short and old, said, "Today, I'll be reading from a book called *The Legends*." He paused, then pulled out a book so torn and dusty it could have been from the medieval days! It had a *D* on it, surrounded by multicolored dots. Jake felt a strange chill up his spine. Mr. Kawigoober began reading from the book. He opened it, then a white flash erupted out of the book.

"The family of Light shall rise again," said an unusual voice. Mr. Kawigoober cleared his throat and looked at the words as though nothing happened.

"The—"

But he was interrupted by the "WOAH!" from the class as they watched a strong gust of wind knock down a thick tree.

Mr. Kawigoober began to say, "Students, calm—" but was again interrupted by a burst of very strong wind and mini tornadoes, water flowing up to two and a half feet, flames erupting on a dry wall, causing holes, an earthquake, thunder, purple fog, and a cold breeze.

"Evacuate, go to—"

But Mr. Kawigoober was interrupted a third time because the ceiling fell in. Purple fog swept into the mouth of a student. Her eyes glowed purple, then she collapsed.

"Suffer in consequence of the departing the ten crystals!" said a voice.

"No, no, no, I . . . I didn't mean to! Elementians, please forgive me!" yelled Mr. Kawigoober.

"You have recited the spell too early. The Legends Ceremony must not take place yet! Isn't it obvious that the book will recite the spell, as it's called *The Legends*? The Dijenuks must rise once more to stop your mistake! Suffer now, and let your city be tortured by the rage of the Elements!" said another strange voice.

Jake turned to David with fear in his eyes. "Did the crazy voice just say Dijenuk?" David nodded.

"RUN!" Jake yelled as the class rushed toward the door or holes in the walls. Gerardo jumped in front of them.

"Curse the enemy!" he yelled. The two cousins shot backward like bullets, feeling sharp pain. Gerardo ran outside with the two following him. David and Jake burst out of the door and ran outside. The school was in total destruction.

"NO!" yelled Jake in complete anger and sadness. It was because he had left a feather of a rare bird in his locker.

Jake, who was in rage, yelled a lot, and somehow, a twister formed under the school, and it spun away from view.

Suddenly, the city exploded. Well, more like blasted off the ground by a huge tornado. Unlike the school, the city hovered there because the tornado kept holding it up.

"AAHH!" everyone yelled. David ran to the right. Luckily, they were close to the city border. Jake ran behind David. When they got there, it was too late to peek over. Some kind of monster made of tornadoes grabbed Jake and David. The strange part was the Wind Giant wasn't solid. Jake and David screamed; just then a voice yelled, "OI!"

A boy, who looked like he was fifteen, was hovering in the air. He held out his hand as though he wanted to dance with the giant and get crushed somehow, and said, "Release them!" But obviously, the giant didn't release David and Jake.

The guy, who still had his hand out, strangely said, "Then take this!" and straightened out his arm more as if he was expecting something to come out, but nothing did.

"What the? Why isn't—AAAAARRGH!" The Wind Giant had let go of Jake and David to whack the boy unconscious. So now the three were falling to their doom.

"This can't be happening," said David in a frightened voice. As they were getting closer to the ground, David and Jake fainted . . .

Jake was in a tunnel. It was very narrow and was very old. Jake heard voices. He heard yells that sounded a lot like him and David. There were bangs and explosions. His dream faded. And then he heard a strange noise, and he awoke again still miles from the ground. Then he heard a bang, and he spun into nothingness, fainting once more.

What had Gerardo done that made David and Jake fly backward? Who was the family of Light? Why was Seattle being destroyed? Why did the strange voice say "Dijenuks"? Who was that flying boy?

CHAPTER 3

Camp Dijenuk

Jake was looking over stone ruins that has bodies all along the floor and three men wearing black suits looking over them. He saw himself unconscious on the floor. The other Jake trembled, as though he were having a nightmare. In his hands was a long wooden pole. David was also on the floor with a wooden pole, except this one had a glowing orb. The world faded, and he saw a war zone. It was an empty field with just dirt and muddy rocks. People were fighting but not with guns or swords—with something Jake couldn't make out. It was very blurry, unlike the stone ruins. Jake didn't notice that he was standing in the sky . . .

"Oi, get up, you."

Jake opened his eyes. He was looking at a tall man in his thirties with blond hair and blue eyes. David was standing next to him.

"What happened?" Jake muttered.

David answered. "Elfekot here"—he gestured to the man—"saw us falling and 'teleported' us to this camp," said David as he added finger quotes to the word *teleported*. "By the way, where exactly are we?" asked David.

"In Elektia, the other version of Earth, and we are in a small town called Camp Dijenuk, which looks a lot like a camp. It also holds the shrine, so it's the most important town in Elektia."

Jake stayed silent for a while, then said, "Wait. Camp *Dijenuk*. As in *Dijenuk* being our last name!" shouted Jake, as though the other things didn't confuse him. Elfekot nodded.

David, who had noticed this too, said, "Get up, Jake." Jake completely forgot about his surroundings. He was lying on some kind of hospital bed in a tent, with other beds around him too.

"Okay, so tell me—is this a joke?" Jake asked Elfekot. No one paid attention to him.

"Can we look around this town?" asked David. Elfekot nodded again. Jake and David stepped out of the tent. Camp Dijenuk was a giant clearing surrounded by trees. The people were wearing light-brown robes with their names sewn on. On the robes were a black *D*, and around it were multicolored dots. "They are weird people," muttered David.

That was because all of them had blond hair and blue eyes. The only way to tell them apart was by their name tags on their robes. The name tags had names that were different from names back on Earth. No William, Harold, Lily, or Bob. There were a few of those kinds of names but mostly strange ones.

In the center of the camp (or town) were pedestals that each shone a different color, the same color on the people's robes. Each pedestal also had a unique hole shape. The pedestals, which were cylindrical, had a symbol carved in the stone. The pedestal that glowed green in the hole had a tornado symbol. The blue one, a drop of water; the red, fire; purple, an eye; brown, a rock—things like that.

The pedestals formed a circle. In the center of what appeared to be a shrine was a giant *D* shining a yellowish gold color. The *D* stood for *Dijenuk*, just like on the people's robes. Also, the multicolored dots stood for the shrine. The pedestals all stood on a slab of stone about the size of a small table, so they could be carried.

There were also many skinny paths that probably led to another clearing or part of the town. Apart from tents, there were also small buildings and cottages, it was as though David and Jake had stepped through a time portal to the medieval days.

The ground was dirt. Cobblestone lined the skinny paths. Logs were also spread around the ground like stepping stones. The logs were also in piles—perhaps for either the campfire that was not lit because it was morning or for the fun of it.

The strangest thing of all was that the people were all carrying long, thin, smooth wooden poles—some with special tops, such as orbs, or special designs. Jake and David had no idea what to say. The people around were surprised too at how they looked and how the town looked as well. "Umm . . . David, we are not in Seattle anymore."

"I see that. What country to do you think this is?" asked David.

"I have no idea, but they speak English, so an unknown part in the UK, USA, or some other place that speaks English. And also, why is the sun blue?" Jake asked David.

The sun above them was not the same yellow-orange of citrus fruits but, instead, an indigo-blue. Strangely, the colored sun emitted bright yellow light, much brighter than the real sun.

"Um, maybe it's the end of the world?" David joked.

"Is that Elfekot man right about being in a planet called Elektia?" Jake asked, because this strange place was popping a million questions into their heads.

David merely shrugged. "No, it can't be. I know there are other planets with life on them but just not this way!"

The book Mr. Kawigoober had opened had a large *D* on it, just like the shrine in the town as well as the robes on the other people. The town was also called Camp Dijenuk. The voices at the school talked to Mr. Kawigoober about the family of Light; David and Jake had no family but each other. The voices also said that the Legends Ceremony needed the family of Light. Jake and David had a strong feeling that the Dijenuks were the family of Light.

But if they were the family of Light (whatever that was), they had to know what exactly was going on and what to do to stop all the chaos and return to Seattle, Washington, USA. If not, then they would be stuck in this strange land forever. Something told David and Jake that they had more important things to do than get home.

Dear reader, think of the time when you saw something strange. How was it compared to David and Jake?

CHAPTER 4

Training

"So all these people are blond?" asked David.

"Yes, obviously, David," said Jake.

Elfekot joined the two. "It's time to start training." David and Jake looked confused. "You still don't know, eh?" said Elfekot glumly. "Well, you two are the last descendants of the Dijenuk family. Your stepparents know it. They also know you are mages of all Elements. You can summon them and use them. That's why the Dijenuk family is worshipped—because you can use *all* Elements. Only you can retrieve the Elemental Crystals to restore the Elements for mages to defend us during the war," said Elfekot.

"Well, I don't believe this Element joke, and this is just an act," said Jake sharply. "Besides, that guy who tried to save me and David didn't use any Elements," Jake rolled his eyes at the word *Elements*.

David sighed. "I believe, Jake. That explains that Wind Giant and the destruction of the city. Fire, Water, Wind! It all makes sense, Jake!"

Jake, similar to David, sighed and walked back in the tent. It annoyed Jake how David believed things really easily, like when their math teacher had said, "All numbers are like letters," as a really bad math joke. David had followed and ended up getting an F in math instead of a D or C.

Elfekot started talking again. "Your city was destroyed because Barbeck Wakigoober opened the book titled *The Legends*—a book that has been written many years ago. It's supposed to bind the Elements together to stay in the shrine, where the Elemental energy emits all over Elektia. It even works on other planets like Earth, and it was supposed to stay closed for twelve more years until Wakigoober opened it. When that happened, the Elemental

Crystals teleported to their temples where Elemental energy cannot emit. They were not supposed to return to their temples until the time was right. Because of this, destruction came because Elements hold the universe together. We must find them before our enemies, the Dark Army and Dark mages, do.

"If they do, then they will use it in something called the Dark Shrine, which will emit Elemental energy only to the Dark mages, but our shrine does it to all of Elektia."

David thought about it. "Okay, complex—but I get it, but why do we have to do it?" David asked.

"Because only the Dijenuk family can access the temples and use all Elements without burning up. So, training—follow me, and don't bring Jake."

David followed Elfekot without saying anything. Lots of people stared at David because he was the only one who did not have blond hair and blue eyes. He had flat black hair and brown eyes. Jake had ovalish green glasses and brown hair and brown eyes.

They entered another large clearing. Near the center of the clearing was a building that towered over the others. It was four stories high with no windows.

Elfekot and David stepped inside the building, which was empty except for a teenage boy who was reading a thick book. Wooden poles hung all over the walls along with targets and big rocks.

"Hey, you're the guy who tried to save me and my cousin from that Wind Giant," David said to him.

"Yes, I forgot that the Elements are unusable. My name is Paul, by the way. I'm a Wind mage here. You must be David Dijenuk. Nice to meet you," said Paul.

"Paul, you must leave. David is going to start training," said Elfekot, while Paul nodded and left.

Elfekot walked up to a wall. On the wall were hanging what looked like wooden poles. "Here, a trainee staff." Elfekot tossed to David a wooden pole, which was a staff. When David caught it, his fingers felt tingly.

"Now, put your right hand on the middle of the staff. Point your staff at the target on the wall. Then summon your energy inside you, and let it flow to your staff. Finally, let the energy blast off the tip of your staff!"

David tried to summon his energy but couldn't. David tried a second time and felt something flow from his chest to his arm to his staff. Later, after about three seconds of focusing, there was a crack like a firework. A shapeless white form appeared out of nowhere and blasted the target.

Elfekot clapped, and as he was doing this, Jake stepped in, looking glum.

"David, let's leave. It's all non—AAAHH!" David blasted Jake off his feet, making him soar backward and smack the wall. David admired his new powers.

Jake closed his eyes and opened them. Then he started yelling. "Why would you—wait, how did you do that?"

"Well, I'm a mage, and I have a staff," said David.

Jake shook his head. "David, there's got to be some trick to that," said Jake, who tried to force the staff out of David's hands.

"Hey, let go!" yelled David. CRACK!

Jake soared upward and landed on his face. He got up and said, "All right, Elfekot, hand me a staff." Elfekot gave him the same one as David. It took Jake much longer than David to learn to blast.

After that, David and Jake learned more moves with their staffs. The Staff Pound—you jump and slam your staff on the ground, creating a powerful force used to knock enemies backward. The Staff Swing—you charge your staff and use it as a sword. And the final move they learned was the Energy Rope. It's used to grab objects such as boulders and logs.

They had also learned that the first Element they were going to find was the Wind Element. Next was Fire, then Water, then Spirit, then Lightning, then Earth, then Ice, then Imagination, then finally, Light. Also, three wars had been planned. They were the First War, Second War, and the Third War. The Light side was fighting the Dark side. Also, Energy and Spell were additional options for mages. Each mage had a power of one of the Elements, as well as limited power with Energy and Spell. There were some Energy-and-Spell mages, giving them full power to both.

David and Jake were tired, so Elfekot led them to their house. It had a fridge, a sixty-inch flat-screen TV, and a bathroom. Their beds were comfortable, and they slept peacefully.

The next day, David and Jake put on their robes and went to training. They were supposed to master the Energy Rope. As they both tried to lift a crate full of anvils, Jake was sweating.

"Why am I so . . . tired?" asked Jake, and David just shrugged.

"Maybe you need to be athletic?" asked David back.

Jake scowled.

David held his staff and raised the crate of anvils. A white rope shot out of the tip of David's staff and reached the crate, making it glow white as well. It stayed five meters in the air for a few seconds, then slowly dropped to the ground.

Elfekot came over to them. "Nice job, David. There is another move you might want to master. It is a little hard. It will suck up a lot of your energy. It's called the Sizzling Crack. It's like a modified version of a blast. You let your energy flow to your staff, but this time, you hold the energy at the tip of your staff instead. You hold it there for a few seconds and then let it out."

David held up his staff. He aimed at a target and let his energy flow to the tip of his staff. A white orb appeared, and David held it there for about six seconds and then let it out. A large blast shot out of his staff and hit the target. BOOM! Wood flew across the room, along with David, Jake, and Elfekot. They hit the wall and fell to the floor. Jake and Elfekot got up. David was still on the floor, grunting. He felt really tired, and his head was buzzing.

"Are you all right, David?" asked Jake.

"I'm fine," David muttered. Elfekot spoke some words, and David twitched. He felt awake, and his head stopped hurting.

David got up. BANG! The three turned around. Elfekot dashed out of the room. David and Jake followed. They stopped. Mages in black robes were invading Camp Dijenuk. They were being attacked by Dark mages.

CHAPTER 5

Invasion And Capture

BANG! CRACK! David and Jake ran to the main clearing to join the fight. When they got there, a mage flew past them.

"It's them Dijenuks!" yelled a Dark mage as he blasted another mage away. David pointed his staff at the Dark mage. BOOM! He fell unconscious.

"David, Jake, protect the shrine!" yelled Elfekot as he blasted Dark mages like crazy. The Dijenuks ran to the shrine, and two mages and Elfekot were already there. Suddenly, about twenty Dark mages surrounded them. CRACK! A Light mage fell to the floor. CRACKLE! BANG! BOOM! CRACK! The four fell unconscious.

David opened his eyes. He was tied up and being dragged across a very long and wide bridge that was leading to a towering castle. In front of them and at their back were Dark mages. To David's left was Jake; to his right was Elfekot. The other two mages were probably left at Camp Dijenuk.

When they were about half a mile away, somebody yelled "STOP!" The Dark mages in front of them got out of the way to reveal a tall man. "Today, we have captured the final descendants of the Dijenuk family. Today, we will make a difference to Elektia. Today, we will finally kill the Dijenuks!" There was a huge cheer from the Dark mages. David looked at the sky. It was black and purple, and he felt himself grow weak and slowly die. "Starting with you," said the man as he pointed his staff at David. A black light started glowing at the tip. "Now . . . suffer and die!" BANG!

Paul was flying over them. He had blasted the man off the bridge. Paul blasted a couple more and landed and untied them. "Now, let's run!" yelled Paul.

"Wait, our staffs!" said Jake as he grabbed their staffs, which hung on a knocked-out Dark mage's belt. He gave the staffs to David and Elfekot and said, "Okay, now let's run!" Paul started flying again and David, Jake, and Elfekot ran across the bridge.

The group was blocked by a gate that had a padlock. David shot out of his staff not a blast but a silver *D*. The gate burst open, and Paul was on the other side, waiting for them. "Let's go!" Paul yelled. Elfekot slammed his staff onto the ground. The four delved into nothingness.

They landed on their faces. Jake got up first and noticed they were in Camp Dijenuk. The rest got up.

"How did we get here?" asked David, who was rubbing his eyes.

"I teleported us to Camp Dijenuk," said Elfekot.

"Oh no," said Jake. The rest suddenly knew what he was talking about. Camp Dijenuk was in total destruction. There were no mages in sight. Camps were on fire. Wood, dust, rubble, and blood littered the floor.

"The town is destroyed," whispered Paul.

Elfekot picked up a staff that had a green orb on its tip. "Take it, David. Opening a Dark Gate is pretty advanced magic for a trainee." Elfekot gave it to him. Then, out of nowhere, Elfekot yelled, "The shrine!" Elfekot ran to the area where the shrine was. "It's gone!" he yelled. The others caught up to him and gasped. It was all bad. The shrine . . . it was gone.

"Wait—don't they need their own shrine?" asked David, but Elfekot shook his head.

"They want to make sure we don't summon the Elements to all of Elektia."

CHAPTER 6

Fight Or Defend

David was quickly thinking. "Maybe we could invade a Dark camp and get it back or something," said David, worried.

Elfekot shook his head. "I don't know exactly where it is. The best chance we have is the Dark camp that's closest to us. By the looks of it, they have just left and probably haven't gone far. The Dark mages who captured us were definitely going a different way from the shrine. We better get moving then."

Paul looked around and then saw something. "Elfekot, there is still the bank and a couple tents left. If we leave, the Dark mages will come and steal all the gold. I have a feeling they are on their way. We either have to fight them or defend Camp Dijenuk again."

Elfekot paced the ground. "Then we'll have to split up—me and David, and Paul and Jake." The rest agreed. About half an hour later, they departed.

As David admired his staff, Elfekot looked at a map. "We go straight for two miles and then turn right," said Elfekot. "Do you remember the signal when we're in trouble?" Elfekot asked David.

"Yeah, shoot a blast in the sky to signal Jake and Paul," answered David. In an hour and a half, they halted. Elfekot looked around. "HIT THE FLOOR!" yelled Elfekot, and they jumped onto the ground. BANG! ZIP! David got up and pointed his staff at a Dark mage. CRACK! ZIP! Elfekot started fighting too.

After knocking out about six Dark mages, they continued. "Judging by the noise we made, they know we are coming," said Elfekot worryingly.

"Well, we've got to keep going. We need the shrine," said David, who was not as panicked as Elfekot. Twenty minutes later, they reached the Dark camp. It was just a thin log wall with a single campfire and a few tents.

BANG! ZIP! BOOM! The two started fighting as they walked slowly into the Dark camp. David did a Crackling Blast that tired him out. CRACKLE! BOOM! A Dark mage flew backward. David noticed that Elfekot wasn't next to him. "Elfekot, where are you?" David saw him next to the shrine. When Elfekot got closer to the shrine, he yelled in triumph. BANG! Elfekot fell unconscious. David panicked; it was just him versus what looked like twenty Dark mages. David pointed his staff at the sky. BOOM! David ran to Elfekot. "Get up—there are too many for me to handle—get up!"

Elfekot still lay there. David pointed his staff at the sky. BOOM! The loudest noise David had ever heard knocked all the Dark mages backward. David got exhausted and fainted.

Jake witnessed David and Elfekot leave. Jake thought the two wouldn't make it. So he just talked to Paul. "I'm not sure they can survive. Don't you think we should go with them?"

Paul shook his head. "No, they are fine." A long time later, Paul looked at a path. He raised his staff. BOOM! A Dark mage fell backward. ZIP! CRACKLE!

Jake noticed they were there. BANG! ZIP! "Paul, they are too many," yelled Jake. Jake shot another blast. CRACK!

Three Dark mages pointed their staffs at Jake. Jake wanted to block it, but he wasn't good at magic. Suddenly, there was a distant BOOM! Jake, Paul, and the Dark mages looked up. There was a blast in the sky. "They are in trouble!" Jake yelled. SIZZLE! CRACK! Jake fell to the floor. Paul panicked. The Dark mages were about to blast Paul, but there was an even louder BOOM! The Dark mages ran back to their camp. Paul ran after them but stopped. As soon as the *boom* happened, Jake blacked out.

Paul looked at Jake. He sighed and picked him up with his staff (Energy Rope), then ran as fast as he could toward the Dark mages. Paul couldn't believe it. Jake got knocked out about the same time David or Elfekot shot the signal. What was that loud *boom*? Could it have been an explosion with staffs? *Probably not*, Paul thought. When he reached the Dark camp, he gasped. Everybody there was on the floor, either unconscious or dead. Jake awoke.

"Put me down, Paul!" yelled Jake, who was surprised to see himself in midair. Paul dropped Jake like an ugly chewed-up toy. When Jake got up, he walked with Paul. They stopped at David and Elfekot's bodies. "Are they dead?" asked Jake with a tone that said *oh no!*

Paul shook his head. "No, David fainted, and Elfekot got blasted. I just don't know how the Dark mages fell unconscious if David and Elfekot fainted."

Jake thought for a while. "What about that huge blast I heard before I blacked out? It might have been Elfekot."

Paul shook his head. "No, it couldn't have been. Elfekot might be an Energy mage, but he doesn't have *that* much power," Paul responded immediately.

"What about David? He's really good at magic. Plus, he got a new staff," stated Jake.

"Well, actually, Elfekot found it on the floor," Paul interrupted. "David is just a beginner mage. Anyway, we must take them back to the camp. It's too dangerous here."

Jake and Paul picked up David and Elfekot with Energy Rope (Jake had some trouble), and they marched to the camp. Right at that point, Elfekot awoke. "Put me down! Don't forget the shrine!" yelled Elfekot, as though nothing happened and he wasn't surprised that Jake and Paul had come. Paul let Elfekot go. He rushed and picked up the beanbag-sized shrine and ran back to Camp Dijenuk.

Paul followed Elfekot and left Jake alone with David.

"I need help. Hello . . . anybody?" Jake called out. His Energy Rope flickered like a lightbulb. David fell to the floor. Suddenly, there was a voice behind David and Jake.

"Welcome back."

Jake turned around. There was a Dark mage that looked strangely familiar. He pointed his long staff at him. BOOM!

CHAPTER 7

Captured Again

It was the worst that could happen to Jake and David. *Captured two times in one day in a strange world called Elektia,* thought Jake as he lay on a prisonlike bed in a prisonlike room. In the room next to his was David, who was still unconscious. Jake thought about his stepparents for a while, then fell asleep . . .

"You try to stop me, fool!" said a harsh voice of a man. The darkness of the room hid his face. Behind him were Dark mages.

"I'll do what I can to stop people like you from getting the Fire Crystal," said a voice that sounded like Paul.

"You leave me no choice but to kill you," said the man. Paul and the man both raised their staffs.

Before the man could do anything, Paul said something poem-like that didn't rhyme. *"Oh, the mages of Elektia, fending for themselves, let this sacrifice, you well!"* There was a blast and then an explosion. Dark mages and Paul lay dead on the floor.

"NO!" Jake yelled. Then everything went black.

Jake woke up covered in sweat. He could not believe what he had just seen. Then he remembered that they weren't supposed to get the Fire Crystal yet. He was after the Wind Crystal, which was green and shaped like a cone. So what did Jake see? Was it a vision or simply a nightmare? Jake got out of his prison bed. He was going to escape. Luckily, since he had kept a magnet that he used for science class, he summoned energy (Paul said you could even without a staff, but it shouldn't be used for combat) to his magnet and used it on the wall. Magically, the wall opened for him.

As Jake stepped into the hallway, he heard a voice. "Jake, what are you doing?"

Jake turned around. David was looking at him. Somehow, David had escaped too.

"I'm trying to bust us out, obviously. Anyway, how did you get out?"

David's staff flashed onto his hands. When David noticed Jake's confused face, he said, "My staff comes with Auto Pack. So if I faint or I'm unconscious or if the staff feels that I don't need it, it flashes away. When I need it, I can summon it using my mind. The Dark mages were too stupid to notice my staff had Auto Pack because it's obvious that my staff wasn't in my hand or, at least, somewhere in that darn place."

Jake was about to respond when there was a yell. BOOM! The blast barely missed Jake.

"Get down!" David yelled.

Jake did what he said as David blasted Dark mages. As the fight moved on, David started looking weary again. Jake came up with an idea. "Hey, David, I could summon energy to this magnet to make some kind of force field to—hey!"

David took the magnet that Jake had powered up from his hands and threw it at the mob of Dark mages. CRACKLE! BOOM! The magnet exploded with the force of a regular grenade.

"That was my favorite magnet!" yelled Jake.

"It doesn't matter!" David yelled back as he ran down the dark hallway. Jake followed.

They opened a small door that led outside. Unfortunately, there were still walls. But worst of all, in the middle of the room was a battle ax and a tall flat rock with bloodstains. Dark mages entered behind them.

David raised his staff. "I learned this spell in some book," he said to Jake. David started chanting. "*Oh, the mages of Elektia*—OUCH!" Jake had slapped David very painfully. "Why did you do—" BOOM! Dark mages had finally decided to blast them. David raised his staff again. CRACK! Three Dark mages were blasted backward. David still tried to hold them off, but it was too late, and there was no way out.

Jake looked around. "Aha!" Jake ran to a piece of stone lying on the ground. He summoned his energy to it and threw it at the wall. BOOM! The wall exploded, causing a hole to appear. David and Jake ran through it, only to see another dead end.

David raised his staff once more to seal the hole before any Dark mages could reach them. They turned around to the wall to look closely at a symbol on it. It was a slightly curved green line. David scowled. "If only there was a way OUT of here!" David started yelling some more when Jake noticed something.

"David, your staff is glowing," he said cautiously. David stopped yelling and looked at his own staff. The tip was glowing like an alarm, except much more slowly. David waved his staff close to the wall, and it started beeping quickly.

Jake got frightened. David touched the wall with his staff. Immediately, the small symbol multiplied to more squiggly lines.

Jake gasped. "The subsymbol of Wind." Jake immediately pulled out sheets of paper from his pocket. He stared at them and then gasped again. "David, this place is connected to the Wind Temple."

David touched the wall with his staff again. Symbols appeared above it.

Jake looked at them for a while. Then he said, *"Oh, mighty rulers of Elektia, release this seal, broken by the Dijenuks."* The ground trembled. The wall disappeared. A long hallway appeared in front of them.

David looked at Jake in awe and fright. Jake gave him a face that said *simple.* David and Jake stepped in the hallway. As soon as they did, the wall closed. In front of them was a small stone table with a scroll on top. David walked toward it slowly. He plucked it from the table and covered his ears for an explosion. When nothing happened, David yelled in triumph. They both ran out of the room but then realized something. "Jake, how do we escape?"

Jake shook his head. "Maybe, umm, we could read that scroll for now."

David nodded and opened the scroll and read, "The Wind Temple is located where thinking looms." David got mad. "Great, we get a poem instead of directions?"

Jake shrugged. "Now we just need to find a way to escape."

David nodded and blew the other wall behind him open. David turned and said, "We're captured again!" The Dark mage grabbed David and Jake by the necks and said, "Give me the scroll." David shook his head and threw it at the sky.

The man got mad and threw them near the rock. At that time, David flashed his staff away. The man walked toward them and picked up the ax. Then he swung it at David's neck.

CHAPTER 8

Visions

As the ax swung through the air, Jake thought everything just suddenly went in slow motion. There was triumph on the ax man's face, fright on David's. The walls blew up once more, Dark mages charged through, mages attacked, the ax man was blasted backward, and a battle began. David got up and flashed his staff back. He went through the door they first came from; a while later, David came back and gave Jake his staff.

Jake grinned and said, "Finally, you thought about my staff." David shrugged and blasted some baddies. Jake joined in the fight too, though he didn't do as well. After five minutes of reckless fighting, Elfekot and Paul arrived. That's when the Dark mages got really frightened, and some even fled.

David ran to Elfekot and Paul and yelled at them, "Why would you just ditch us like that, Paul? I almost got my head chopped off!" As Elfekot calmed David down, the fight started going badly. More advanced Dark mages arrived. Three mages got seriously injured. Jake got tired and panted for a long time. David motioned for Elfekot to follow him to cover. David flashed the scroll into his hand. Elfekot's eyes grew to large circles.

Elfekot stammered until he finally was able to speak. "Is that the Scroll of Wind? Where did you find it?"

David laughed. "Yeah, I found it on the opposite side of the wall. I have no clue what it means."

Elfekot opened the scroll and looked at it. "You're right, I don't know what 'where thinking looms' means. We must start finding the Wind Crystal.

There are a few more scrolls out there that might help us find the Wind Chamber."

David nodded. "For now, let's fight these guys and leave this place."

Elfekot and David got up and started to trap Dark mages with Energy Rope. As they fought, David realized something. More of the Dark arrived, and David got mad and slammed his staff on the floor. Elfekot thought he did this in anger. But he was just fighting with energy. A circle of energy appeared around David. It started closing in on David, and when it did, a beam of energy shot out of David's staff, causing at least five Dark mages to be blasted backward, right through the walls.

Jake looked at David. "Wow, you really are talented at magic." David grinned and kept doing that until he collapsed. Elfekot and Jake rushed toward him.

"He used too much advanced magic. Oh, I have an idea!" said Jake as he pulled out a sheet of paper from his pocket. Jake started reading it. *"Switch the energy from me to David Paluktus Dijenuk."* Immediately, energy flowed from Jake's chest to David. As David got up, Jake fainted.

When David stood up, he looked at Jake confusingly. "What happened?" asked David.

"Well, Jake used a spell that transferred his energy to you. Jake must be a good Spell mage. He probably gave up his energy because you are better at magic than he is." Elfekot said.

David agreed.

David thought that there was something odd about Jake. He looked like he was having a nightmare. You couldn't have a nightmare if you were unconscious. David shrugged and rejoined the fight once more.

A man was standing in front of Jake. But the man wasn't looking at him. In fact, it was like he wasn't there. The man was looking down from a cliff. Jake walked to see what the man was looking at. An army of at least a thousand Dark mages were marching toward a forest. The forest looked a lot like the place where Camp Dijenuk was hidden.

As soon as they reached the forest, there were blasts and fire and water everywhere. Mages from every town in Elektia were running toward the great city, trying to protect it.

Jake looked at the man in horror and lunged at him. But Jake went right through him, as though he were a ghost. Jake kept trying but decided to look at what was happening. Forest trees were burned down or forced off the ground. Mages were blasted back and forth. Blood was everywhere. The Dark mages were succeeding, though it was hard to tell due to the large crowd. Suddenly there were blasts of tornadoes, fireballs flying, and waves of water. The Dark mages were frightened. Half of them lay on the floor.

The man scowled. "I'll handle him, fools!" The man took out his staff and jumped down the cliff.

Jake's vision dissolved and reappeared. This time, though, he was floating over a fight. The man was battling David. He shot puffs of black smoke; David blocked the attacks with a yellow shield. Jake looked closely at David; he looked older. David looked like a ninth grader holding a staff and shooting blasts. Except he wasn't blasting; he was shooting yellow glowing balls as well as miniature tornadoes. David couldn't be using Wind and Light. Jake and David hadn't gotten any Elemental Crystals yet.

Jake tried to pull out his staff to help but couldn't. He looked at himself and screamed. He was transparent. So he tried to sum up what happened before he fainted. Jake had transferred energy to David and fell into a coma. That didn't help, so Jake thought of what happened before *that*.

Jake had escaped out of his cell along with David, who still had his staff. They had gone out into an outside room with an ax and a bloody stump. They had opened the walls and found a scroll that made no sense. The Dark mage had been about to chop off David's head, but the mages, Paul, and Elfekot came. Jake gasped. Paul was alive. He thought he had seen in his dream that Paul had died. So that meant it was a nightmare or . . . Jake had visions! Jake was proud of his special powers until he realized that this would happen to Camp Dijenuk in the future.

Jake panicked and looked at the city. Tents were burned to the floor into ashes. Buildings were on fire. More importantly, the shrine was being guarded by Jake himself.

Jake got confused as he looked at himself chant spells and blast off Dark mages. Jake looked back at the main fight.

The man kept yelling at David. "Fool, why do you keep fighting me? I'm the king's top mage—you should be blasted to dust!" The man made a huge ball of some kind of energy that Jake thought was the evil element, Dark.

David barely blocked it with his magical golden Light shield. His shield flickered and disappeared.

The man laughed. "Ha! Now, do you surrender, boy? If not, you're gonna need a coffin."

David grinned. "I'll keep fighting till I can't fight." The man was about to blast David when Jake's vision dissolved.

CHAPTER 9

Government And Third Capture

Jake's eyes snapped open. At first, he thought all the mages had put on suits. But when he got up and looked around, the Dark mages, Elfekot, David, Paul, and the other mages were twitching on the ground as though electrified. Jake felt the ground for his glasses, and once he found them, he put them on and noticed what was happening.

The men in suits were Men-in-Black. They were walking around the unconscious and dead bodies. As they walked and talked silently, Jake thought he saw garbage on the floor. Jake looked more closely and saw rubble, blood, broken staffs, and bits of robes. Jake groaned which was a mistake. The Men-in-Black heard and walked toward him. They pulled out a Taser and said, "You're coming with us."

Jake grabbed his staff and said his best spell. *"Curse the Enemy."* All three of them yelled in pain and shot backward.

Jake jumped up as more Men-in-Black rushed toward him, and one of them tased Jake. Jake screamed and stumbled backward. *"Curse the Enemy!"* Nothing happened, and more Men-in-Black ran toward him like tiger catching a prey. *"Curse the Enemy! Curse the Enemy!"* Still, nothing happened as the Men-in-Black loomed closer and Jake grew weaker. *"CURSE THE ENEMY!"*

All Men-in-Black were blasted backward. All but one who snuck up behind Jake and punched him on the back.

Jake woke up with a shiver as he noticed he was in a spacious but cold room with David, Elfekot, Paul, and other mages who survived the battle. *Not again*, thought Jake.

David walked up to him. "While you were unconscious, the mage fought for our lives. Later, the government came and electrified us while ye were still unconscious. Now, we are in Area 51! What happened to you before you woke?"

Jake thought about it and told him about the skill he had just learned he had and his vision. "After I got up, I tried to fight of the government, but I got knocked out."

David chuckled. "Wow, visions? I read in some book that very few mages can have visions. I am also not surprised you got beaten by them."

Jake got annoyed. "I use *Spell* magic, David, not Energy magic. In case you don't know what that means, it's magic that uses chants. Some are short, some long. The one I used was *Curse the Enemy.*"

Paul came over to them. "Stop fighting, you two. Since we're trapped, we should try to get out before bad things happen." Paul's prediction was right. When David was about to say something back to Paul, the door opened and two men came in.

"All right, all of you, come with us." The mages followed them outside when David shouted out, *"FIRE!"* There was a rumble as fire erupted from David's hand and flew throughout the area. David went chasing after them. The mages followed David.

David went inside a room filled with staffs, scrolls, books, and other things mages could have. David took his staff and the first Wind Scroll. He ran back out with the other mages and blasted people out of his way. Both Dark and Light teamed up to fight out of Area 51. David yelled *"Water!"* and like the fire he summoned, a wave of water swept the Men-in-Black away. David flew in the air and flew back down to use a powerful Staff Pound. Slowly, the mages moved along, causing destruction and alarming the Men-in-Black.

David was the main amazement of the battle. He stood in the middle of a room filled with fighter jets. Jake thought David was fighting too many by himself and went to aid him. A Dark mage passed, fighting an old man with murder in his eyes. Jake yelled, "Fight them, don't kill them. *Curse the Enemy!*" The Dark mage screamed in pain as more Dark mages came.

Light mages came to aid Jake. When David had handled his mini-fight, he came to help Jake. David used a Sizzling Crack and knocked out three Dark mages and two Men-in-Black.

Paul ran to Jake and David and said, "We're fighting the Dark mages and the normal humans. We can't hold them off for long."

Jake agreed, but David said, "We got to try!"

David ran off to fight the Dark mages, blasting every one of them. Jake sighed and went to join David. David yelled, *"Imagination!"* David thought about a horse stampede. Immediately, horses appeared out of nowhere and charged at the Dark mages.

David got tired quickly after his summon. Elfekot ran to him. "Stop using Elemental Magic! Without the Elemental Crystals, you could kill yourself!"

David said nothing and kept panting.

Elfekot jogged, dashing back to aid Jake and the Light mages.

David coughed a bit, and when he thought he could faint, there was an explosion, and David flew through the air. Voices rang in his head as David fell to the floor.

"David, stop . . . stop fighting . . . you know you can't win." David recognized the voice as his father and Jake's uncle. "Stop . . . please stop this foolery . . . you don't have to join us, David Dijenuk . . . for your father . . . don't let the same thing happen to you . . . give up . . . there's no hope. You don't have to keep fighting . . . You can end all of this . . . just stop."

CHAPTER 10

The Fight Of Area 51

David stood on the floor, tears running down his cheek like a leaking pipe. David stood up with shaking legs, then fell to the floor and threw up.

Elfekot ran to him, blood running down his arm. "David, are you sick? It might be too much magic for you."

David shook his head. "I—I heard something . . . in my head, I think."

Jake ran to him. "David . . . I think I heard my dad."

David felt as if he was going to throw up again.

Those voices sounded fake but so real at the same time. They were dead, so it must have been one of the Dark's tricks. There were a lot of spells and powers David and Jake didn't know yet. If the Dark did do those tricks, then why? The explosion had already knocked some sense out of David and Jake, it could have created horrifying voices in their heads as everything went in slow motion.

The two had a feeling that they would hear more voices soon.

Jake looked sick as well. Paul came over. "Hey, we're still fighting, you know!"

Elfekot looked at him angrily. "The Dijenuks are sick for some reason. Show some respect!"

Paul was slightly frightened but later joined the jumble of staffs and Tasers that was the battlefield. Some government officials had fled, and alarms were ringing. David suddenly remembered something. "Jake, maybe you can have a vision!" said David.

Jake brightened and took a deep breath. Nothing happened. David raised his staff and blasted Jake, knocking him out. "Maybe that'll give him a good vision." Elfekot made a magical shield with his staff to protect David and the knocked-out Jake from any harm.

Elfekot ran out to battle but stopped and said, "Use no more Elements. They're not doing you" He continued and reached the battle.

As Elfekot fought, David thought about the previous events. When an explosion had occurred, David had heard a voice as he flew through the air. Everything had gone in slow motion. The voice had talked about giving up.

David thought more thoroughly. *Maybe it was just an illusion.* David thought it was probably that and lie down to rest.

There were more explosions, a chunk of the ceiling collapsed, and staffs were flying everywhere like someone was playing volleyball with multiple balls. Elfekot and Paul were still fighting in a lively manner but most of the mages (both Dark and Light) were tired and were eventually knocked out.

Jake opened his eyes to see a heavily destroyed room. Voices rang through the room like echoes.

"I can't believe I sent some of my best mages out only to get killed! They were captured by mortals!" The voice wasn't full of guilt; it was full of blame.

"My king, I am sure that this won't happen again! I know it's my fault that we lost. But I killed Jake!"

The king still looked angry. "What about that David kid? He hammered a large number of our mages! He'll only get better!"

Jake looked around. He recognized the room as Area 51 . . .

Jake opened his eyes and gasped. He was going to get killed! Jake looked at the battle. The man who was going to kill him was fighting three Light mages. "David, that man over there is going to kill me!"

David looked at the man Jake was pointing at. David ran out of the magical shield and fought his way toward the man. He did the move he used at the prison courtyard. David slammed his staff on the ground; he let the energy fly out from his staff, and it charged the energy back up.

David let out a burst of energy. The man blocked it with a small magical shield. He couldn't hold it for long, so he was blasted backward. The man got up and ran through a hole in the wall and across the hot desert. David ran after him. Elfekot noticed and ran after *him.*

Meanwhile, Jake was relieved that his whole fate was changed just because of a vision. David chased the man, and Elfekot ran after David. Jake got up and stepped out of the shield. Immediately, Dark mages pointed their staffs at Jake. *Oh, not again!* Jake thought. The blasts caused Jake to be knocked out for the seventh time.

Paul ran toward him. "Great, David and Elfekot left the battle, and now Jake is unconscious!" Paul walked away, but not too far in order to protect

Jake. There was another explosion. All three teams—the few government officials, and the Light and Dark—were split apart by the blast.

A man in dark robes appeared in the middle of the group "Some of you might know me, some of you don't. My name is Landor, the king of Dark. Why won't we stop fighting? All teams had a great loss, except mine, of course. I'm still here. Not David or Jake. Yes, the moment I've been waiting for. There are one thousand of my men out there. So hand over the two Dijenuks."

One of the Light mages said, "David is chasing a Dark mage down. You'll never find him!"

Landor smiled. "I see that you're hiding the Dijenuks, but you don't stand a chance! MAGES . . . ATTACK!"

So, reader, what do you think will happen next? Are you sure you want to continue? If you do, then go and read the next chapter.

CHAPTER 11

Finally Starting

So, are you ready to hear what will happen next? Good luck, reader.

Dark mages charged through the walls. Immediately, the Light mages all yelled, *"Dijenuks' Curse!"* The staffs created a large ball of energy. The energy exploded, sending all the Dark mages flying backward. The spell caused the Light mages to disappear—all except Jake, who was under a pile of rubble.

David ran through the desert as though he was a cheetah. The man ran farther and farther away until David couldn't catch up. He stopped and panted. David looked at the man who was stuck alongside a cliff. David walked slowly toward him until the man noticed and grabbed David by the neck. "So, you think you can get me? Well, probably not at the bottom of a cliff." The man threw David into the pit.

Jake awoke once more with pain on his right arm. Jake pushed the chunks of ceiling off him. Jake saw that the room was completely empty. Jake went outside into the boiling desert. "WHERE ARE YOU GUYS?" yelled Jake. Jake went inside the building to pick up his staff and the scroll that David had dropped during the explosion.

Jake went back outside and felt his staff vibrate. As he walked around, his staff vibrated harder. When the staff vibrated enough to give Jake more pain, he dropped it. Jake's staff blew all the sand surrounding it away, revealing the wind symbol. Jake muttered *"Winds of the glory,"* and the symbol disappeared, causing a hole to open nearby. Jake fell in the hole and landed safely in water.

Jake got up and saw a stone door. There were symbols on it that Jake could read. Jake read them out loud. "Welcome to the Wind Chamber, Dijenuk." Jake knew exactly where he was.

David got closer and closer to the ground where he thought he would shatter like glass. David hit the ground with an unusual soft thud. He got up and saw an old man grinning. David gasped. "Uncle Bertank!"

Bertank smiled. "I have been hiding here for years, thinking I was the last Dijenuk standing, until I heard about the Dijenuks on the Elektia news channel."

David was surprised to see his uncle. He had thought Bertank had died of cancer. "What happened to you, Uncle Bertank?"

Bertank chuckled. "Your parents lived in a house near Seattle, but then the Dark invaded the Dijenuks' house and killed them. When your parents died, the Dark mages looked around for more Dijenuks. Meanwhile, I was trying to find a home for you and your cousin Jake. I found one and explained it all to them. By the way, where is Jake?"

David shrugged, and Bertank looked worried.

David suddenly had a huge question in mind. "Uncle, is it possible for mortals to enter Elektia? Because we were captured by some, and now I'm on Earth."

Bertank got a serious look on his face. "Sometimes, mortals accidentally step into Elektia and get all confused. It also happens with mages. I had to step into Earth to keep you two safe. I was kidnapped, and I escaped into Earth. Sometimes, things from Elektia vanish into Earth. Like the Wind Chamber. That's one of the hardest Elements to find if you're after them."

David's mind cleared. Bertank spoke again. "I'm hiding here to guard the entrance to the Wind Chamber. You need all three Wind Scrolls. There's another entrance near this place, but no one knows how to open it. Luckily, I'm guarding the Wind Chamber, and I have a scroll, and so do the Dark mages."

David didn't know if this was good news or bad news. The Dark mages had one, his uncle had one, and he had one. "Uncle, I left a scroll at Area 51, which is really close to here."

Bertank nodded and picked up his staff. *"Float the ally!"* David hovered in the air and then soared upward like a rocket. David reached the sand and was dropped off at the edge of the cliff.

David ran toward the building and went inside. He noticed it was empty except for Elfekot. He was sitting on a pile of rubble. "David, I ran after you, then I heard something in this building. I went here and saw someone fall in a hole. Maybe it was Jake."

David knew that Jake was at the second entrance of the Wind Chamber. David nodded. "Yeah, it probably was Jake. By the way, have you seen the Wind Scroll?"

Elfekot shook his head. "You lost it? Now we can't get in the Wind Chamber. Guess we'll have to find it. Anyway, what happened to you?"

David decided to keep everything about his uncle to himself. "I found the entrance to the Wind Chamber."

Elfekot had a victorious look on his face. "Now we need three Wind Scrolls. Can you show me where the entrance is?" David nodded and decided to show him Bertank anyway.

As the two walked across the steaming desert, David thought about everything that had happened. First, he had been captured with Jake at a camp. Paul and Elfekot had taken the shrine to Camp Dijenuk. It had looked like afternoon, and when he had woken up at a prison, it was morning. It was afternoon again when he had been caught by government. Now it was afternoon once more, so he hadn't eaten for two days. David's stomach growled when he thought about food.

When David and Elfekot reached the cliff, Elfekot looked confused. "We have to go down there?"

David couldn't believe it either. "Yeah, the entrance is down there. Strange, it's so close." David jumped down into the pit. Elfekot, who was very unsure, jumped down after him.

David fell to the ground without any pain. Elfekot came down a couple of seconds later. David never noticed the TV, kitchen, and bedroom in the pit. David also didn't know that magic could turn into electricity.

"So, David, where is the entrance to the chamber?"

David said nothing and looked around for Bertank. Elfekot followed David, then said, "David, is this a joke?" David found a stone door and opened it. They both stepped into the foul-smelling bathroom. "David, does someone live here?" David still didn't say anything as he looked around once more.

When David entered what looked like a closet, he screamed. Bertank Dijenuk lay dead on the sandy floor.

CHAPTER 12

The Second Scroll

Elfekot had no idea what was going on. "David, who is this?"

David half responded and half sobbed. "That m-m-man is m-m-my Uncle Bertank!"

Elfekot didn't believe him. "David, there are no remaining Dijenuks left—ahhh!" David's anger had struck Elfekot, sending him flying backward.

"He is my uncle. I remembered last seeing him when I was three years old!" said David, crying. "When he took us to a home, he had thought we would have died later. So he was surprised to see me. Jake didn't even get to see him!" David ran away to hide his tears. Elfekot yelled at him to come back, but it was no use.

As David ran, he stopped. David had thought he had heard whispering. David ran once more. As Elfekot watched David flee, he noticed a note sticking out of Bertank's pocket. It read,

> David, the Dark mages have a scroll. Jake has one. The entrance to
> the Wind Chamber is under the

The rest of the note wasn't written down. Elfekot sighed. After a couple of seconds, he heard David's voice. "No, I won't. It will never happen!" Elfekot darted toward the direction David had run. When Elfekot found David, he sat on the floor with eyes filled with horror. "I heard my dad's voice over at Area 51. This time, I heard my Uncle Bertank's voice."

Jake woke up with an aching head. He had gotten bored in the hole and slept on the softest piece of land he could find. Jake was very hungry, so he had eaten some grass. Jake got up and looked at the door. "Why won't this door open? Doesn't it know I'm a Dijenuk?" Jake sighed and lay down once more to sleep. A voice ran through his head.

"I'm your and David's uncle, Jake. Don't be afraid to hear my voice. Now, do what I say. You must stop looking for the Wind Crystal. I know you have a scroll, but I also know that you are hungry and tired. The Light mages have fled Earth, and they are now in Elektia. So, Jake, you must go home, continue your normal life . . ." Jake knew what that voice was. It was Bertank Dijenuk's voice.

Jake knew that he must not give up. But he was hungry and tired. Jake remembered in their days of training that he could use an Energy Rope as a grappling hook. Jake picked up his staff and summoned his energy. An invisible rope shot out of Jake's staff and through the hole. Jake went up and reached the ground. Jake didn't know what to do next. Jake remembered that Elfekot had slammed his staff on the ground and teleported them to Camp Dijenuk.

Jake wanted to teleport home to see his stepparents. But he had to continue. Jake picked up his wooden staff and slammed it onto the ground. BANG! Unlike the first time he was captured where he had felt nothing at all, Jake now felt like sinking into the ground at an extreme speed. After what felt like minutes, Jake hit the dusty ground of Camp Dijenuk. He got up and looked at the shrine. It stood in a glass case on a stone pillar. Its gray color matched the smoke from the destroyed buildings as mages repaired Camp Dijenuk, the most important city in Elektia.

Jake still couldn't believe that this small city could hold the most important object in Elektia. The mages had finally noticed Jake's arrival. Paul came over to him. "You must be hungry. Come, we have some food left." Paul took Jake to his and David's tent.

Paul made hot broth along with a glass of water. "Eat—you need to recover if you want to find the Wind Chamber."

Jake remembered what he had discovered. "I found the entrance to the Wind Chamber."

Paul had a relieved look in his face.

"Yeah, I'm a bit excited too. Anyway, here's the first scroll."

Paul took it and said, "Good, that's one. Elfekot contacted me and said he was going to look for the remaining scrolls here in Elektia. He says the Dark mages have it. I'm not worried though. Now that you could have found the entrance, we will soon go into that chamber!"

Jake didn't want to say it, but he did anyway. "I don't know how to open the entrance!"

Paul's relieved face turned into a face of desperation. "Well, I know we'll find a way. For now, just rest, and David and Elfekot will get the two scrolls back. I know they will. Both of them are experts at magic. You're an expert at Spell magic. I noticed."

David walked silently across the soft ground. Elfekot opened a portal into Elektia. David still hadn't told Elfekot what he had heard in the desert. He knew that his uncle or his father would tell him to give up. The two went to the city of Virtane. They ate at a diner and rented a room in a hotel. Elfekot got one room; David got another. David's room had one bed, a small table, a bathroom, a closet, and a flat-screen TV.

The next day, Elfekot and David had breakfast at the hotel. As David ate a bowl of cereal, someone burst into the room. "I have a package for David Dijenuk!" The man gave David a lumpy package. The man bowed, then left respectfully. David read the note on the package.

To David Dijenuk

From Scott and Oka Stert

Things are tough here on Earth; we can't get food or electricity. Don't worry. Everything will be fine. We sent you this gift from Earth to Elektia. We sent Jake a similar package.

Inside the package was a scrapbook. He opened it and looked at the photos of him, Jake, and his stepparents. His summer vacations, his birthdays, and other special times. David looked at his class photo. He looked at his best friend, Wilbur. Wilbur and the rest must be wondering where he was and what had happened during the city's destruction.

Elfekot watched him sadly. "You must miss the mortals. Maybe you'll see them again."

David wasn't sure. David put the scrapbook on the table and looked at the rest of the package. There was a bag of his favorite candy, Jolly Ranchers, and a sculpture he had made. It was a copper sphere-shaped object. It had the words *David's Masterpiece* engraved perfectly onto the smooth copper.

Tears ran down David's cheek once more as he thought of memories back on Earth.

"David, look out the window!" David looked out into the street. Dark mages marched through the town. They carried two scrolls.

"We are sorry for the disturbance of Virtane, but we must use this town to protect two valuable objects."

David and Elfekot went outside quietly.

One brave villager said, "And what if we want to stay?"

The mage who was speaking smiled. "You all must leave, or you all must be killed."

The villager who had spoken said, "Well, this is our town!" The other villagers cheered.

"Well, fighting it is."

The villagers took out their staffs and pointed them at the Dark mages. "Even if we're not soldiers, we can still fight!"

The Dark mages laughed and pulled out their staffs.

David whispered to Elfekot. "We can't let this happen!" The two pulled out their staffs. "Hey, what about us!" David said as he and Elfekot walked in front of the mages. The villagers cheered once more. When they had done this, the fight began. Immediately, there were cries of pain and agony in the air. David and Elfekot fought for Virtane.

David knocked out the Dark mage who was holding a scroll. David took it and said, "I have the second Wind Scroll!" The Dark mages fled when they had heard this, taking the third Wind Scroll. David still had the second one, however.

CHAPTER 13

Time To Team Up Again

David opened the second Wind Scroll as quick as he could. David scowled and threw the Wind Scroll at a wall.

Elfekot picked it up and read it out loud. "The Wind Chamber is both close and far." Elfekot shrugged and said, "Well, at least we have two. We just need to find one more to access the Wind Crystal."

David nodded. "I know that, but I don't know where the entrance is."

Elfekot went back inside and came out with his and David's stuff. David took them. "I wonder what Jake got."

Jake ate breakfast alone, with no one to accompany him. A mage stepped into his tent. "Sorry to interrupt, Jake, but I got a package for you." Jake took it silently. It had brown wrapping, and it was lumpy. Jake read the note attached to it.

To Jake Dijenuk

From Steve and Oka Stert

Ever since you and David left, we have missed you. Because of the tough times here on Earth, it's been hard. I hope this gift will mean a lot to you. I'm not sure when you'll come back.

Jake opened the package quickly yet carefully. Inside was a scrapbook, a bag of his favorite books, and his favorite souvenir from Canada—a T-shirt.

Jake opened the scrapbook slowly. Inside were photographs of family vacations and school events. Jake's tears hit the pages of the scrapbook.

Another mage stepped in, ruining Jake's privacy. "David and Elfekot got the second scroll. They are after the third scroll, which the Dark mages have." Jake put all his stuff into a leather bag, flung it over his shoulder, took his staff, and ran out of the tent.

Paul came up to him. "I know you want to help your cousin, so I'm going with you."

Jake nodded, and he ran with Paul through the forest with thin trees. When they reached the field, Jake was surprised at how the outside of Camp D looked like. He hadn't really paid any attention to it in his vision.

"Okay, if we walk west, we will reach Virtane, where David and Elfekot are. Let's just hope they don't leave before we get there." They continued to walk across a stone path toward Virtane.

Jake pulled out an energy bar out of his pocket and started eating it. "Is there another way to travel?"

Paul nodded. "Yes, but it's powered by the Elements."

Jake groaned. After forty minutes, they reached the small town.

It had buildings like a normal city on Earth, except the names of the buildings and their purposes were different. Jake and Paul saw David and Elfekot walking out of a building that said "The Mage Choice Inn." Jake and Paul ran to them.

"We came just in time. We want to go with you to find the final scroll," said Jake.

"Sure, we have a long journey ahead of us. Let's just hope there are towns along the way where we can eat and restock our supplies. We have gold, and all Dijenuks get everything free, as long as it's not too much," said Elfekot. The four walked through town and back into the lonely fields.

During the walk, David noticed something about Elektia. It had the same animals as Earth—same atmosphere, same plants. The cities, unlike Earth, were split apart by a huge field. When it got dark, Jake used a spell to summon a campsite. It had four tents and a roaring fire.

Elfekot just went to sleep. Paul was outside, gazing at the stars. David lay inside his tent, thinking about his stepparents and friends. Jake sat in his tent, using a flashlight to read a book titled *Basic Spell Magic for Travelers*.

David went outside to join Paul. "Do you have a family with you?"

Paul was a little startled at that question. "Well, my dad died in the Civil War when all of Elektia was split into ten sides for a few years, and my mom divorced my dad, so I live alone," Paul said with difficulty. "I'm gonna go to bed." Paul left David alone outside.

The next morning, Elfekot got up first and woke the others. They got their belongings and kept on walking. When they reached the town of Fentorta, the four ate breakfast at a diner. David and Jake had pancakes, and Elfekot and Paul had omelets.

A man snuck up on Jake and took his leather bag. "Hey, drop my things!" David and Jake ran to chase the thieving man. The thief reached a dead end. David and Jake pulled out their staffs and pointed them at him.

"Before you destroy me, my name is Hegyid." Hegyid pulled out a spell book from Jake's bag. *"Curse the Enemy!"*

David and Jake screamed in pain and fell backward.

Hegyid flipped through the pages. *"Protect me from the foul ones!"*

David used a Sizzling Crack. The attack reflected and hit the two. "Jake, he's got your spell book!"

Jake scowled. "It's obvious because he's got my bag!"

Hegyid said another spell. *"Use the power of the ones in front of me, and use it back!"*

They both felt a strange sensation in their chests. A silver-colored beam appeared out of nowhere, and it aimed at David.

The beam hit the tip of David's staff. David swung his staff like a club, and the beam's power rebounded all around. David got up and looked at Hegyid. David remembered a spell that Jake had used in Area 51. *"Grab the things that aren't his!"* From Hegyid's backpack came out gold, jewelry, and from Hegyid's hands, Jake's bag and spell book.

David caught Jake's things and handed them to Jake. Hegyid got up and used his staff to teleport somewhere else. They returned to the diner and told Elfekot and Paul what had happened. "When I was about to blast Hegyid, he teleported," said David, finishing the story.

Elfekot sighed. "There will be a lot of thieves as we go through Elektia."

Jake got up from the table and said, "Well, we should leave. I know a spell to track Wind Scrolls. Oh, and if we would have never teamed up again, we would have lost the war." The rest stood up, and together, they left the diner. Before Elfekot left, he put some gold on the table.

Jake looked at a map that was in his bag. "All right, we don't need to stay anywhere because the closest town is Hegortant. The *source and key of the wind lies wherever in the dimension,*" Jake chanted. After a moment, Jake said "Okay, we'll head right toward Hegortant." They left the town and went toward Hegortant.

CHAPTER 14

Hegortant

When the four reached Hegortant, villagers clapped. "It's the Dijenuks!" one of them yelled. They reached a hotel. Jake made sure that Hegyid didn't take anything from his bag.

"Why are you checking? I used that spell to take everything he had that was not rightfully his," said David once they reached their hotel room.

"Well, I'm not sure about your Spell magic," Jake responded. Jake pulled out his stepparents' gifts, three spell books, a small bag of gold, two other books, a flashlight, three individually wrapped sandwiches, six energy bars, and a bottle of water.

David was surprised at how much that bag could hold.

"Yep, I got everything," said Jake, relieved because David didn't fail at the spell.

"How can that bag hold all that stuff?" asked David, bewildered.

"I used a spell," Jake responded.

The two cousins heard yelling. "You might as well walk out this door and yell 'Hey, Dijenuks, we got the third scroll!' We cannot alarm the Dijenuks!" said an unfamiliar voice.

"We've got to pull an explosion off! That way, in all the confusion, we can sneak away with Elfekot and Paul! Then when the Dijenuks notice and come after them—we capture the Dijenuks, steal the scrolls, and we win!" screamed another voice.

The yelling stopped, and they heard footsteps. "Jake, let's go!" panicked David.

The Dijenuks left their room and went out into the street. In front of them were two men in dark robes. David pulled out his staff and did a Sizzling Crack. BANG! The Dark mage flew backward. His partner turned around and muttered a spell. David and Jake felt a pain in their insides.

They ran toward the Dark mage and suddenly received an electrical shock. Pain seared the Dijenuks' insides. They lay on the floor in pain, groaning. The other mage got up.

"Curse the Enemy!" yelled Jake. The Dark mage collapsed to the floor once more. The still-standing Dark mage used another electrical shock on the Dijenuks.

Jake's muscles clenched and squeezed. David flew a couple yards upward and fell back down. David got up first and held his staff tightly and swung his fist. Another larger, glowing fist appeared out of nowhere and smacked the Dark mage, knocking him into a coma.

The second Dark mage got up again and pulled out his staff. Jake lazily knocked him out with a simple spell. They noticed a very large sack on the floor. David opened the sack. Inside were Elfekot and Paul, their chests soaked with blood.

"It was a trap . . . they don't have the third scroll . . ." whispered David.

"Elfekot . . . Paul!" Jake muttered. "I hear their pulse!" Jake cheered up.

"Hey, Jake, do you know a spell that can awaken them?" asked David.

"No, I don't," Jake responded.

"I can't believe that would happen. At least they are alive," David pointed out. They took Elfekot and Paul to their hotel room. In about two hours, Elfekot and Paul got up.

"I hate those Dark mages! I want to find those scrolls quick so I can restore my Element," Paul said, a little dizzy.

"They snuck into our rooms and attacked us. They looked tough," said Elfekot to David and Jake, who were startled to see them up.

"Well . . . we are glad you are alive. Anyway, I searched the Dark mages' pockets, and I found a note that said the third scroll is under Hegortant!" said David.

"Well, what are we waiting for? Let's ask the villagers if there are any underground tunnels," said Jake enthusiastically.

The four ran out of the hotel room and into the lobby. It was a heated room with red carpet. A wooden counter was in a corner, and chairs and sofas lined the walls. There was a flat-screen TV on the wall. Two women sat on chairs, sleeping. A man was arguing with the bellboy. Elfekot cleared his throat loudly. "Excuse me, does anyone know about any underground tunnels?" The two women snapped awake, and the two arguing men turned toward Elfekot. They just laughed.

"Oh, great," muttered Paul.

"Let's speed things up, shall we?" said David. He pulled out his staff. BOOM! David blasted a hole in the floor.

"David!" screamed Jake. The villagers froze in fear. The four mages peeked into the hole.

"Whoa," whispered David. Inside the hole was a dim room. Elfekot, Paul, Jake, and David climbed down a ladder. The hole was fairly deep. "I noticed that the floor sounded hollow," remarked David. About half a second later, the floor of the hotel fixed itself, leaving the room as dark as the night sky.

Jake muttered something. A very bright ball of light appeared before their eyes.

"Staffs out," whispered David. The other three did as told. They heard footsteps in the distance. Suddenly, the ball of light disappeared. They heard more footsteps, then a click. A hard blow hit David in the chin. He fell to the ground with a thud. There was a click, then another thud. Two more clicks, and two more thuds. There was a grunt, more footsteps, and another click. There was screaming in the distance and a noise that sounded like a human getting shocked.

The ball of light reappeared. Jake, Paul, and Elfekot were also on the floor.

"What was that?" said David.

"I think it was . . . meant to scare people," said Jake.

They looked at their surroundings. There were shelves stuffed with books and notes cluttering tables. Jake grabbed everything on the shelves and tables and put it in his bag. The walls were made out of rock and dirt. There was one tunnel that led down, deeper into the earth's surface. Jake whispered a spell, and all the torches in the tunnel were illuminated.

They entered the tunnel, which was as damp as a swamp. After about five minutes of walking down, they found a large room, which was lit by torches. Shelves crammed the walls, which held scrolls.

"Which one of these is the third scroll?" asked Elfekot.

"Should Jake have a vision? Just to see which one of these is the right one, in case it's a trap," said David.

Jake sighed. "Fine, but how are you—"

David knocked Jake out with a hard rock on the floor.

Jake felt himself floating. Jake heard screaming, so he opened his eyes. The tunnel was on fire. So were the scrolls. There was more screaming. Jake awoke.

"Which one is it?" said David.

"None of them," said Jake. Jake walked a couple steps backward and then opened a hidden door in the ceiling. The third Scroll of Wind popped out. Jake caught it. The four cheered.

"Now we need to go back to Earth, go back to Area 51, and find the entrance to the Wind Chamber!" exclaimed David.

They heard clapping. "Well, well, well, how nice to see you again, Dijenuks." It was Landor, king of the Dark mages. "Now . . . give me the scroll!"

Z-CRACK! Landor flew backward. Dark mages suddenly came through the tunnel. Landor shot a black fog at David. He started to choke as though it were poisonous fog. "*Curse the Enemy!*" Landor shot backward once more. The Dark mages shot blasts and so did Elfekot and Paul.

"Jake and Iwill take Landor," said David. David shot powerful blasts at Landor, and Jake muttered spells. Landor kept blocking their attacks.

Paul and Elfekot assaulted the Dark mages. BANG! BOOM! CRACK! Dark mages kept swarming endlessly. ZIP!

"ARRGH!" Paul was hit by a blast in the shoulder. Blood soaked his robes. "Elfekot, I'm hit!"

Z-CRACK! Elfekot got blasted in the legs. Elfekot fell to the floor. Paul sat against the wall. The Dark mages loomed closer. BANG! Jake and David both shot a blast at Landor, which he reflected onto the ceiling, causing it to fall. In the confusion, Jake and David ran out of the tunnel and blasted the ceiling. They climbed out the tunnel and dashed out of the hotel.

Jake and David kept running until they were a long distance from Hegortant.

"What about . . . Elfekot and . . . Paul?" panted David.

"I guess . . . we'll . . . have to . . . go without them."

They trudged back to Camp Dijenuk.

"I haven't seen this place in a while!" said David. They entered their tent and looked at the third scroll. "Memories and the past are things to think about." David thought about it. "That's definitely Uncle Bertank's home."

Jake was confused. "Who's Uncle Bertank?"

David stared at his feet. "Um . . . he was one of the last Dijenuks remaining, and he got killed."

Jake froze and said nothing.

They stayed at Camp Dijenuk for a couple of hours, thinking about ways of getting to Earth. "We could go into space and somehow get to Earth," said David.

"David, we are on the other side of the Milky Way galaxy—that's a stupid idea!"

David sighed and continued skimming books. "How did you get to Elektia?" David asked.

"You can teleport from Earth to Elektia easily. But Elfekot said, sometimes, people accidentally find a portal leading from Earth to Elektia and vice versa," Jake responded.

David nodded and continued to read books, when he heard a loud voice. "Elfekot and Paul are captured! I repeat, Elfekot and Paul are captured!"

The two rushed out. Mages asked the announcer questions. "We've got to save them!" said David. He ran out of Camp Dijenuk. Jake followed him.

The cousins reached Hegortant. The hotel they stayed in was still intact. They stepped in and went inside the tunnels.

"WE WILL NEVER TELL YOU!" It sounded like Elfekot.

"You will tell us!" It was the voice of Landor.

"AHHHH!" They heard Elfekot scream in pain.

Jake and David snuck behind a group of Dark mages. Z-CRACK! David blasted three mages forward.

"*Curse the Enemy.*" Jake used the spell on two Dark mages.

Landor turned around. "Get them, fools!" Dark mages charged forward, blasting the Dijenuks but missing.

"*Protect me from the foul ones!*" An invisible shield appeared around Jake. David kept fighting the mages. ZIP! BANG! Jake's spell caused blasts to reflect and hit Dark mages.

Slowly, the crowd of Dark mages stepped backward, avoiding all the blasts. David charged a blast. BANG! Four Dark mages were knocked out. "*Curse the Enemy!*" Three more Dark mages were shot backward.

Landor got annoyed. "I'll get them!" Landor shot a powerful blast at David. Jake jumped in front of David. BAM!

CHAPTER 15

The Beginning

The blast hit Jake's shield and rebounded, but the force of the blast sent Jake flying backward. The blast hit Landor, and he shot upward. David summoned the last of his strength to summon a blast of wind. Landor flew backward. The wind gathered all the Dark mages along with Landor and shot them through the tunnel's roof and into the sky. David's vision blurred. He buckled, and he blacked out.

David woke up in his bed at his home. Sunshine lit the room like a bright summer day. He got up and looked at his bedroom mirror. He was wearing normal clothing, and he had no staff clipped to his belt. He was just wearing a red polo shirt and some jeans and socks. David opened the door.

Cheerful noises filled David's ears. He walked through the small hallway and down the stairs. His stepparents were talking to Jake about his day at school.

His stepdad, Steve Stert, noticed David first. "Oh hey, buddy, you're a bit late for dinner—your potatoes might be cold."

David walked to the dinner table slowly. "Um . . . what happened?" he asked.

His stepmom, Oka Stert, answered, "Don't you remember? You came home from school and went to your room to take a nap—a long one too."

Her soothing voice always cheered David up on a gloomy day, with her brown hair that was the same color as Jake's and that same cleverness which had people mistakenly think that she was their real mom. Their stepdad, Steve, had brown hair as well but brown eyes. David was about to sit on a chair, but then he got confused. "How did we get back?" David asked.

"What are you talking about, David?" said Jake.

"How did we get back from Elektia?"

Steve chuckled. "You must have had a weird dream, David."

David panicked. "It can't be a dream . . . Jake, you remember Elektia and mages, right?"

Jake shook his head.

"But you have to remember, Jake! We went to Elektia, and we met Elfekot and Paul and . . . the scrolls! Where are they?" David panicked even more.

"David, it was just a dream," said Oka.

"No, no, no, it can't be a dream . . ."

David's eyes snapped open. He was lying on the floor of the tunnel. Light mages were asking Paul and Elfekot questions. Jake was still unconscious. One of the Light mages noticed David get up. "David is awake!" he yelled. The mages cheered. Around the same time, Jake got up as well. "So is Jake!" another mage said. The mages cheered even more. Jake felt dazed, just like David.

The three scrolls were floating in the room. Jake grabbed them and put them in his bag.

There was a distant BOOM. Silence fell upon the mages. A purple fog swept through the tunnels. Landor appeared before their eyes. David jumped to his feet, along with Jake. David summoned his staff into his hands.

Dark mages appeared behind Landor. All the mages, Light and Dark, pulled out their staffs. The two teams were waiting for someone to make the first move.

A Light mage blasted a Dark mage off his feet. There was a split-second moment, then BANG! Blasts flew everywhere, knocking mages out. David kept launching Sizzling Cracks at Dark mages as easily as walking.

Jake kept using spells and curses while reading from a book. Jake then used a spell to suck everybody in the tunnel into the hole David made with Wind. They all landed hard on the ground, not very far from Hegorant. They all got up and kept fighting.

Landor ran toward Jake and David. He shot a purple cloud at David. He felt his soul leaving his body, feeling cold and empty—"*Reject the curse!*" The purple fog turned into a yellow beam, and it shot backward, hitting Landor.

David sat on the ground, grunting. He felt like someone put those vacuum tubes in his mouth and turned it on. Landor got annoyed by the pain, as though a vicious cat had pounced on him multiple times. He raised his metal rod and shot a black beam and drew a circle around him, Jake, and David. Jake tried to run, but when he met the edge of the circle, he flew backward as though there were an invisible shield. David shot Landor with a weak blast, which he blocked.

Jake stood next to David. They both pointed their staffs at Landor. They felt more like brothers instead of cousins. They charged a blast. So did Landor. But the Dijenuks shot first. The blasts from the Dijenuks turned into a solid beam of energy. It hit Landor's staff. But the beam got stronger. Landor couldn't handle the beam. His metal rod vibrated. David and Jake felt tired, but they had to keep going. The force of the beam caused Landor to slowly step back.

Landor hit the invisible shield and dropped his rod. The beam hit Landor and shot backward through the shield. He hit the ground like an anvil coming from an airplane. The Dark mages saw what happened to their king and turned into black smoke. The smoke disappeared. Jake and David fell to the floor.

David and Jake woke up at about the same time. They were in their beds at Camp Dijenuk. They got off the beds.

Elfekot entered the room. "Good job, you two. Landor is injured, so we won't hear from them for a while. Now that we have all the scrolls, we can enter the Wind Chamber. But we need to get back to Earth and find the Wind Chamber."

David sighed. "So I guess no magnificent Wind power . . ."

Jake nodded.

Paul entered the tent. "Elfekot, we got a new shipment of staffs—oh, hello, David and Jake. You guys really took him over there."

David nodded. "The Dark mages will recover soon. So we have more work to do. This is only the beginning."

Chapter 16

Good Start

King Landor watched Seattle being destroyed. He had the ability to warp himself and others to Earth. Landor laughed as he watched the Dijenuks fall to their deaths. Maybe he didn't need to plan everything out after all. Suddenly, there was a flash of light, and the Dijenuks, as well as the other boy, were gone. Landor didn't mind much though, as he had planned everything out.

Landor's battle partner, Allen, was standing next to him, watching Seattle being crunched by everything. "What do we do with the city, my king?" asked Allen.

"Once we get the Wind Crystal, the tornado and all other Wind curses will stop, and Seattle will be on the ground once more. We will take it over as the start of our empire on Earth, and I'm making you king of Earth. I'll still be the ruler in general, of course," said Landor.

"Thank you, my king," said Allen.

"I'll put your castle in the middle of the city. I'll call it . . . New Dark's End. You know, because my palace is in Dark's End, and this is New Dark's End," said Landor.

Allen nodded.

"It's time to get back to Dark's End. We have a lot to do, Allen." The two disappeared into thin air.

They reappeared at Elektia with a BANG! They were in Landor's palace at Dark's End, the capital city of the Dark. Landor sat on his throne. "Allen, prepare the attack. Tomorrow, Camp Dijenuk will be attacked, and my plan will succeed!" said Landor, excited.

Allen nodded and left the throne room. In about twenty minutes, he came back with a large group of Dark mages.

One of them spoke. "I am the leader of Sector 38 in the Dark side, guarding the—" started the man, but King Landor interrupted. "I don't care much about your sector. I just want you to attack Camp Dijenuk tomorrow. Capture the Dijenuks. They have just arrived, and they shouldn't put up too much of a fight. Capture Elfekot as well—he is their friend. They will be the ones guarding the shrine. Take them to your castle and execute them," commanded Landor, who knew that the Dijenuks would escape anyway. "Also, have another group of your men raid the place and take the shrine to the nearest Dark outpost. I'll contact you for further orders later." The group of mages nodded and left.

Landor knew the fight between the Dark and Light would be bloody and brutal. Without the Dijenuks, the Light side would be weakened so much that the Dark could win so easily. The Dijenuks family grew smaller each generation; now it fell to two boys. The Light had no chance. The Landor family was more powerful. Landor thought it was a good start. Once the Dijenuks were out of the way, the Light side would fall, and the Dark would win. It was just a matter of killing them and getting the Elemental Crystals.

Allen spoke again. "So what do we do, my king?" asked Allen.

"I will be on the watch and make sure everything goes as planned. Also, there is something I need to do to make sure the plan works. Allen, you can take care of the Dark side. The messenger will give you a list of things to do while I'm gone. I will only be away for a few days. The final step of my plan is to kill a Dijenuk in hiding named Bertank so I can lure them into a trap. The Dijenuks will be lured into a trap, and I will capture them one last time. I will come back with the Dijenuks' bodies and kill them in front of everyone at Elektia. Let's just hope David and Jake don't separate from each other."

Allen nodded, excited that he would get to be in charge for a few days.

Allen left the room, leaving Landor alone in the throne room. "The plan is going well, and soon I will be the ruler of both Earth and Elektia, said Landor to himself. "The Dijenuks are new to Elektia, and they won't know how to use their powers very well. This will be too easy." Landor left his throne room and went into another room. He was on the balcony, looking over his kingdom. His castle was large, with many towers and rooms. The capital city, Dark's End, was very rich and heavily guarded. Landor already had a lot, and he was going to have more. What if his plans failed? No, Landor couldn't think about that. If the Dijenuks got the Wind Crystal, then Landor had to make a new plan. Landor had taken years to make the current plan. He could not afford to fail. If, somehow, the Dijenuks won all the Elements, then Landor would be back to square one. He had to wait until they were older and kill them when they felt happy and safe, when they got married and had children. Landor just couldn't lose.

ONE DAY LATER . . .

The Dark soldiers marched toward Camp Dijenuk. "All right, here we are men! Our orders are to attack the place and take anything we want! The king also wants some of us to take the shrine and bring it to a nearby outpost. The rest of us will take the two Dijenuks here and bring 'em to our sector and kill 'em there! Let's go, men!" said the leader as the soldiers cheered.

Their group of about eighty stormed through the trees. BANG! BOOM! They blasted mages silly, and one saw two boys step out into the main area of the camp. "It's them Dijenuks!" yelled one.

David and Jake ran toward the shrine. Some of the mages attacked them. CRACK! CRACKLE! BANG! BOOM! CRACK! The group of mages, along with David and Jake, fell to the floor.

"You guys and I will take 'em to our sector! The rest—you all will grab the shrine and bring it to that outpost nearby!" said the leader.

About fifteen mages took the bodies and disappeared into thin air. The rest raided the camp and took almost everything.

"Run to the emergency hideout!" yelled one of the Light mages. They scurried around and left the camp. The rest of the Dark mages left with the shrine.

Landor stood on top of a tree, watching them. "Good, it's working." Landor disappeared into thin air. Landor reappeared in another sector and watched the Dark mages and their speech. Suddenly, a flying boy appeared and blasted the mages, saving David, Jake, and Elfekot, who went back to Camp Dijenuk.

Everything else went as planned, until David and Jake found one of the Wind Scrolls. He had forgotten that the Wind Scroll was at the prison. At least Landor knew where the other two were.

After days, Landor returned to his castle with anger on his face.

"My king, you have returned," said Allen.

Landor said nothing. Instead, he walked to his bedroom, furious at his defeat. "The Fire Crystal is next. That one I have to win. I can get the Wind Crystal too if . . ." said Landor to himself. Landor smiled, then laughed. "This is only the beginning, Dijenuks."

END OF BOOK 1

Edwards Brothers Malloy
Thorofare, NJ USA
June 7, 2013